This book belongs to

★ ⋯⋯⋯⋯⋯⋯⋯⋯⋯⋯⋯⋯⋯⋯⋯⋯⋯⋯⋯⋯⋯⋯ ★

Written by Nick Ellsworth
Illustrated by Michelle White
Designed by Chris Fraser at Page to Page

This is a Parragon Book
This edition published in 2005
Queen Street House
4 Queen Street
Bath
BA1 1HE

Printed in China.
ISBN: 1-40541-020-5

Twinkle
the
TOOTH FAIRY

Written by Nick Ellsworth ★ Illustrated by Michelle White

p

Twinkle the Tooth Fairy says...

Look after your milk teeth. Brush them in the morning and before you go to bed. If you have the chance, brush your teeth after meals, too.

Brush round and round, and inside and out.

When one of your milk teeth starts to wobble, it's getting ready to come out. Once it has fallen out, save it for me! Put it in your special tooth purse under your pillow, so that it's easy for me to find.

While you are asleep, I will leave a coin in its place for you to find in the morning!

In time, another tooth will grow to replace your milk tooth. Remember to brush your new teeth carefully too.

Twinkle
x

Twinkle the Tooth Fairy was always very busy. Every night, she collected the milk teeth that the children left under their pillows. But the teeth were so tiny, that they were difficult to find in the dark.

Late one summer's evening, she was looking for the last milk tooth.

"It must be here somewhere," she thought, tip-toeing around the edge of the bed.

Suddenly, she saw something sparkle in the moonlight. The tiny tooth had fallen on the floor! She picked it up carefully, and put her last shiny coin under the pillow.

"Goodnight," whispered Twinkle as she gently kissed the sleeping child and flew silently out of the window.

The sun was just coming up as Twinkle flew back to Fairyland.
All the fairies were very busy getting ready for the Fairy Ball.

Fairy food had
to be made
by the best
fairy cooks.

Hundreds of
fairy lights
had to be put up.

And the fairy
orchestra was
practising very
hard to make
this the best
Fairy Ball ever.

Before going to bed, Twinkle decided to
go and see her friend Thimble, the fairy
dressmaker. Thimble had been busy
too, making all the dresses for the
Fairy Ball.

"What beautiful dresses!"
exclaimed Twinkle.

"I'm glad you like them," said
Thimble. "But they would be so
much better if I could decorate
them with golden thread. I can't
find any in the whole of Fairyland."

"I know where there's lots of
golden thread. Leave it to me,"
Twinkle said excitedly, and flew off high
into the sky.

She flew higher and
higher. Soon, she was
among hundreds of
bright, shining stars.
On she flew, until
she reached a huge
golden ball – the Sun.
"Please, Sun," she
asked, "can you spare
some of your fine
golden thread for my
friend Thimble? She
needs it to make her
dresses for the
Fairy Ball."

Twinkle waited. All of a sudden, a long trail of golden thread came
slowly from the centre of the Sun. Twinkle took the end of it,
and began to pull it towards her.
"Ooh, that tickles," laughed the Sun.
Soon, Twinkle had gathered a large bundle of the precious thread.

"Thank you, Sun. Your thread will make my friend Thimble very happy."
"You're very welcome, Twinkle," chuckled the Sun.
Then she flew back to Fairyland, being very careful not to drop
the golden thread on the way.

When Thimble saw what Twinkle had brought her, she clapped her hands with joy!

"Thank you, Twinkle. Now my dresses will look perfect! And you will wear the finest one at the Fairy Ball."

"I've never been to the Fairy Ball," said Twinkle quietly.

"Why ever not?" asked Thimble.

"It takes me such a long time to find all the children's teeth, I never get back in time," she said sadly.

"Don't you worry. I'll think of something!" said Thimble. Twinkle felt very tired after her busy night and went straight to bed.

When Twinkle woke up the next day, she was surprised to see a large bag at the foot of her bed. Inside the bag were the most beautiful purple and gold velvet purses.

"I wonder what these are for," she thought. Pinned to the bag was a note, which read...

Dear Twinkle,

I have made these special purses from the left-over fairy dress cloth. The children can put their teeth into them. The purses will be much easier for you to find in the dark. With a bit of luck, you will be back in time for the Ball!

Your best fairy friend,

Thimble
x

Later that evening, Twinkle
collected all the children's
milk teeth as usual.
She left each child with a
shiny coin tucked into one
of the purses, which she
carefully placed under their
pillows. She whispered to
each sleeping child,
"Please use your new purse
to keep your next milk tooth
safe under your pillow."
When she had finished her
night's work, she flew back
home to sleep.

The night of the Fairy Ball had come at last! Everyone had travelled far and wide to be there.

Twinkle was very excited,
and hoped that she'd be back in time to join in the fun.
But first she had her important job to do.

When she flew off that night to collect the milk
teeth, Twinkle was overjoyed to see that each
child had put their milk tooth inside
their purse. Now, they were easy to find!

She kissed each
child and whispered,
"Thank you!"

After gathering them all up
carefully, Twinkle flew quickly
back to Fairyland.

When she was nearly
home, Twinkle could
hear the sounds of
the fairy orchestra in
the distance.
The whole sky was lit
up from the lights of
the Fairy Ball.
"Oh no! It's already
started," she thought.
So she flew even
faster.

When she reached home, Twinkle rushed to see her friend Thimble.

"Am I too late?" she asked breathlessly.

"It's only just begun!" laughed Thimble. "You're in plenty of time." Thimble gave Twinkle one of her beautiful dresses to wear. While she was dressing, Twinkle told Thimble all about the good children putting their milk teeth in their new purses.

Twinkle had a wonderful time at the Fairy Ball,
and ate the most delicious fairy food she'd ever tasted.

Twinkle danced for
hours, and didn't feel
in the least bit tired.
And everyone agreed
that in her beautiful
new dress, she was the
prettiest fairy of all.